D1191793

THE CHURCH MICE AND THE RING

Graham Oakley

ATHENEUM 1992 NEW YORK

Maxwell Macmillan International
NEW YORK OXFORD SINGAPORE SYDNEY

Atheneum
Macmillan Publishing Company
866 Third Avenue
New York, NY 10022

Library of Congress Cataloging-in-Publication Data

Oakley, Graham.
The church mice and the ring/Graham Oakley.—1st ed.
p.   cm.
First published in Great Britain, 1992, by Pan Macmillan
Children's Books.
Summary: The church mice carry out a convoluted plan to
find a home for their new friend Percy, a stray dog.
ISBN 0–689–31790–5
[1. Mice—Fiction.   2. Dogs—Fiction.]   I. Title.
PZ7.01048Cfc   1992
[E]—dc20   91–45273

Macmillan Publishing Company is part of
the Maxwell Communication Group of Companies.

First edition

Printed in Hong Kong

10 9 8 7 6 5 4 3 2 1

It was a nice day, so Humphrey was taking the opportunity to point out to everybody the hole in the ozone layer. But since holes in nothingness aren't all *that* interesting to look at, when Sampson hove into view most of the mice rushed off and shouted rude remarks at him just to liven things up a bit.

Sampson didn't mind because he was used to mice being rude to him, but then he spotted something he jolly well did mind.

After the mice had calmed Sampson down they got chatting to the stranger.

He told them that his name was Percy and that as a puppy he'd been a Christmas present and that things had been really nice. The trouble was, he said, people who liked puppies don't always turn out to be people who like dogs, so, to cut a long story short, he was now sleeping rough in the churchyard waiting for something to turn up.

Mice know what it's like not to be wanted and they all agreed that he'd better stay in the vestry until he'd got things sorted out.

Sampson didn't think much of that idea and told them so, but Humphrey said that that kind of silly, anti-dog talk was just about all you'd expect from a cat.

"All right," said Sampson, "you'll see."

They did too, that very night at supper time, as they watched Percy gobble their whole week's cheese supply in two minutes flat and then ask what was for pudding.

Next morning in the porch, while Percy was taking a nap, the mice held a conference.

They agreed that if Percy stayed in the vestry, they'd all starve, and though while personally not one of them minded starving in the least, no one could bear to stand by and see a friend starve.

So they put their heads together and came up with a pretty good scheme for finding Percy a new home.

While Humphrey and Arthur got the scheme rolling by making a notice for the newsagent's window, the other mice put together a scratch breakfast from the odds and ends that were thrown over the churchyard wall every night.

Then there was an interruption.

"Sorry," said the girl, "the ball just kind of . . . " Then she saw Percy and forgot everything else.

Humphrey and Arthur recognised love at first sight when they saw it and not being the kind of mice to let such a golden opportunity slip through their fingers they dashed forward with their notice and made such a nuisance of themselves that the girl had to take her eyes off Percy for a moment and read what they'd written.

After she'd read it, Polly, for that was the girl's name, said that her mum and dad had loads and loads of nice things and they'd be jolly pleased to have a really super dog like Percy guarding it all for them.

So they set off for Polly's house feeling very happy that things were working out so well.

When they arrived, they found that Polly's parents had invited a few friends round for a barbecue, so it wasn't the best time for introductions. And it soon got worse.

For one thing, Percy had an attack of nerves and forgot himself, and for another, Sampson and the mice entered into the party spirit a great deal too much for most people's liking.

The upshot of it all was that they were asked to leave and never, ever come back again.

Later that day, Polly called in at the vestry to see them. She said that, after they'd been ordered to leave, her parents told her that she could have a dog but it had to be a really *nice* dog.

"In that case," said Humphrey, "Percy will have to learn how to be a nice dog," and he spent the rest of the day teaching him.

For several days after that Percy prowled around Polly's house and never missed a chance to show her parents that he could do all the things nice dogs do and a few more besides.

He showed them he was *dependable*, by paying them visits every day . . .

and *loving*, by taking them little gifts . . .

and *useful*, by helping Polly's mum weed the garden . . .

and *thoughtful*, by fetching the newspaper for Polly's dad . . .

and *playful*, when the occasion was right . . .

and *FIERCE*, when it came to defending them from intruders.

After a few days, Polly gave them a report on Percy's progress. She said that at first her parents had called Percy "that animal", but since his visits had started they were calling him "that horrid little pest".

It was decided, therefore, that the visits to Polly's parents had better stop – instead, Percy could do something really big and win their hearts in one fell swoop. The only snag was, nobody could think of anything big enough.

However, that afternoon Humphrey and Arthur just happened to overhear Polly's mum telling her friend about her diamond ring. She was saying that it was a family heirloom and that she prized it more than anything else she owned and that if she ever lost it, she just didn't know what she'd do.

The two mice looked at each other . . . and smiled.

Late that night, Arthur, Humphrey and Sampson crept out of the vestry. The bright moonlight made it easy for them to find

Polly's house, and the wisteria and the open bathroom window made it easy for them to climb in.

Then things stopped being easy.

But with the aid of some talcum powder and some spine-chilling moans and some blood-curdling words about being

the ghosts of mice come to wreak vengeance on cats that had eaten them, they managed to get what they came for.

Next morning, they hid the ring outside Polly's house and Humphrey gave Percy his instructions.

"All you've got to do is get Polly's mum and dad out here and show them where you've found the ring."

"Right-o," said Percy and he dashed off.

"Well," said Humphrey while they waited, "unless something unforeseen happens in the next few moments, Percy'll soon be fixed up with a nice comfy home."

They made their way back to the vestry feeling very depressed. Percy was brooding about the terrible things Polly's dad had just said to him and Sampson, and the mice were brooding about the hungry days that lay ahead thanks to Percy still being on their hands.

At that moment Arthur saw something and he drew Humphrey's attention to it. Before they reached home they'd decided that the diamond ring plan was still alive and kicking.

As soon as they were back in the vestry a meeting was held, and Humphrey told them that the slight hitch in plan, which some of them might have noticed that morning, could easily be ironed out. All he needed was a dozen or so brave volunteers prepared to risk life and limb in a bold raid on a jeweller's shop.

For once, all the mice went quiet. So Sampson stepped in and said that anybody whose name began with an A or a B or a C could consider themselves volunteers and if they wanted to argue they knew where they could find him.

So late that night Arthur, Humphrey, Sampson and a sulky band of Anns, Alberts, Brendas, Brians, Clares, Cuthberts, etc., made their way through the deserted streets to the jeweller's shop.

Sampson helped them in and mounted guard ready to give a warning whistle if he saw a policeman coming.

When they were inside, Humphrey made them stand around him and gave them a long talk about how vital it was not to waste a second standing around talking. Then he ordered them to start the search and to make sure there was none of their usual messing about . . .

. . . but he might just as well have saved his breath.

After about half an hour Arthur found the ring. He'd hardly done so when they heard Sampson's warning whistle followed by the sound of heavy footsteps approaching the shop door.

They all froze and held their breaths, but after a few moments the footsteps went away.

The mice started to rush for the back door, but Humphrey stopped them. "That's just what the policeman will expect us to do," he said. "At this moment he'll be plodding around the back ready to nab us as we come out. So what we'll do is we'll leave by the front door and I give you my personal guarantee that the coast will be clear."

After they'd been brought to the police station the sergeant gave them a very severe talking to, but he had ended up by saying that as they were church mice they couldn't be that bad and they'd probably only been playing a foolish prank, so he'd let them off with a caution.

That really hurt Humphrey's feelings. He strode forward and said that if the sergeant couldn't tell the difference between a foolish prank and the operation of a master-mind carried out with clockwork precision, then he was just a rotten old silly-billy.

The sergeant thanked him for pointing out his mistake and had them locked up.

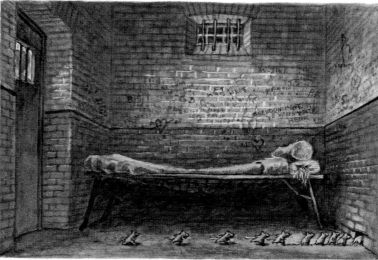

Escaping from the cell was no problem, but they still had to get hold of the ring again.

So Arthur and Humphrey reconnoitred and worked out a plan of action. Then Humphrey asked for volunteers for what he called a "suicide mission". Nobody seemed too keen until

Arthur explained that what Humphrey actually meant by a "suicide mission" was just having a bit of a lark and a few laughs. After that things went as follows:

. . . 11.39 p.m.   . . . 11.40 p.m.   . . . 11.45 p.m.   . . . 11.50 p.m.   . . . 11.55 p.m.   . . . 11.57 p.m.

. . . 11.58 p.m.   . . . 11.59 p.m.   . . . midnight.

Sampson had seen everything, so when the sergeant came out of the police station he was waiting. When he was certain which way the sergeant was going to go he dashed ahead and took up a strategic position. At exactly the right moment, he struck like lightning.

They put the plan into action again on the following Sunday and they'd hardly hidden the ring before Polly's parents arrived for morning service.

But just as Percy was about to "find" the ring his attention was diverted and Polly's mum spotted it herself.

But she'd scarcely found it before she'd lost it again.

That was because the jackdaw who lived in the church tower and loved shiny things got there first.

Then they went up the church tower and the lucky mice who'd managed to hitch a ride chanted "We stole a stole" all the way to the top just to screw up their courage.

It was the last straw for Sampson. He never thought much of the plan and now it seemed a good time to take over the operation.

"Follow me," he snapped in the kind of voice that nobody feels like arguing with.

First they borrowed the parson's stole.

The jackdaw was an old enemy and Sampson had always kept   have taken the ring. He checked, though, to make sure
an eye on him; he had a pretty good idea where he would   and then explained the change of plan to Percy.

Sampson said that a lady like Polly's mum would never have thought very highly of a chap who just found things; daring and panache were more in her line. If she saw Percy risk his life for her, he'd be home and dry.

Percy said that risking lives was all very well for a cat because if he loses one, he's got eight spares, but a chap who's only got one life has to be jolly economical with it.

But deep down Percy knew that Sampson was right, so he did what he was told.

"Pheeeeeeeew!" said Humphrey when they'd come to rest and for once everybody agreed with him.

When Polly's mum saw the ring her heart at last went out to Percy. She said that a person who'd risk his life for a diamond ring was a person after her own heart and welcome to a bean bag under her roof for as long as he liked.

Polly's dad still had reservations about Percy, but they didn't matter very much because what Polly's mum said went.

Everything had worked out well. Sampson and the church mice felt a warm glow in their hearts because they'd helped to find a good home for a poor waif and they felt an even warmer glow in their stomachs because they knew that from now on that poor waif wouldn't be hogging everything they had in their larder.